The Stinky Giant

First published in 2009
by Wayland

This paperback edition published in 2010 by Wayland

Text copyright © Karen Wallace 2009
Illustration copyright © Cathy Brett 2009

Wayland
338 Euston Road
London NW1 3BH

Wayland Australia
Level 17/207 Kent Street
Sydney, NSW 2000

Series Editor: Louise John
Cover design: Paul Cherrill
Design: D.R.ink
Consultant: Shirley Bickler

A CIP catalogue record for this book is available from the British Library.

ISBN 9780750256049 (hbk)
ISBN 9780750258166 (pbk)

Printed in China

Wayland is a division of Hachette Children's Books,
an Hachette UK Company

www.hachette.co.uk

The Stinky Giant

Written by Karen Wallace
Illustrated by Cathy Brett

WAYLAND

Princess PJ lived in a castle beside a big lake. She liked riding her horse, climbing trees and getting dirty. Princess PJ was a tomboy princess!

In the summer Princess PJ went swimming every day.

Sometimes, when no one was looking, she dived off branches into the water.

6

Her brother, Prince Dandyfop, was a bit of a weed. He didn't like swimming at all and hated getting his hair wet.

Queen Clementine said swimming wasn't very ladylike. There was too much shouting and too much splashing.

King Crusty liked swimming but he was very forgetful. One time, he jumped into the water and forgot what to do next!

9

One day a giant arrived at the castle.
Princess PJ opened the door.

"I'm sorry to bother you, but please
may I have a cup of tea?" he asked.
"I've walked a long way and I'm
very thirsty."

Before Princess PJ could reply, Queen
Clementine wrinkled her nose.
"Tell that giant to go away," she
whispered. "He's too stinky."

Prince Dandyfop pulled a face. "His clothes are old and ragged," he sneered.

"But giants tell REALLY good stories,"
said King Crusty.
"All he needs is a bit of a wa..."

Then King Crusty sighed because he had forgotten what he was going to say.

"I won't have a ragged, stinky giant in the castle," said Queen Clementine firmly. "Send him away!"

"Quite right, Mummy," said Prince Dandyfop.

Princess PJ rolled her eyes. Why did she have such a wet lettuce for a brother?

Princess PJ ran to the castle dressmaker. "See that giant," she said, pointing out of the window. "Could you please make him some new clothes?"

"What with?" asked the dressmaker.
"He's enormous!"

"You'll think of something," said Princess
PJ firmly.

Then she filled up a big bottle with water and ran after the giant.

The giant drank the whole lot in one gulp.

"Thank you so much," he said. "One good turn deserves another. What can I do for you?"

"Do you know how to swim?" asked Princess PJ. She knew it was the only way she could make the giant have a wash.

"Of course," said the giant. "Would you like me to teach you?

"Yes please," cried Princess PJ.

After her swimming lesson, Princess PJ
changed into dry clothes.

"You learned very quickly!"
said the giant.

"Well, you're a very good teacher," said
Princess PJ. "Would you like to have
tea with us now?"

The giant shook his head sadly.
"I would love to, but my clothes are
too wet."

"One good turn deserves another,"
said Princess PJ. "I've got a present
for you!"

So the giant put on his new clothes and stayed for tea. Queen Clementine had never heard such wonderful stories. "Tell me the one about the beanstalk again!" she begged.

Prince Dandyfop was amazed. He'd never seen such wonderful clothes! Although he felt sure he'd seen that material somewhere before...

"It's like I've met two giants in one day," Prince Dandyfop said to his sister. "It's extraordinary!"

"Just like a really good story," cried Princess PJ.

She winked at the giant and they both burst out laughing.

START READING is a series of highly enjoyable books for beginner readers. **The books have been carefully graded to match the Book Bands widely used in schools.** This enables readers to be sure they choose books that match their own reading ability.

Look out for the Band colour on the book in our Start Reading logo.

The Bands are:

🔵	Pink Band 1
🔵	Red Band 2
🔵	Yellow Band 3
🔵	Blue Band 4
🔵	Green Band 5
🔵	Orange Band 6
🔵	Turquoise Band 7
🔵	Purple Band 8
🔵	Gold Band 9

START READING books can be read independently or shared with an adult. They promote the enjoyment of reading through satisfying stories supported by fun illustrations.

Karen Wallace was brought up in a log cabin in Canada. She has written lots of different books for children and even won a few awards. Karen likes writing funny books because she can laugh at her own jokes! She has two sons and two cats.

Cathy Brett has been scribbling all her life – first on pieces of paper, on walls and sometimes on her sister! She later became a fashion designer and an author/illustrator. Her scribbles have appeared in lots of books, in shop windows and even on beach towels. Cathy likes listening to really loud rock music!